Salámán and Absál

An Allegory

Translated from the Persian of

Jámí

جلال‌الدین محمد رومی

By

Edward FitzGerald

Prefaced and Edited by H.D. Greaves

Jámí's Epitaph

"When your face is hidden from me,
like the moon hidden on a dark night,
I shed stars of tears
and yet my night remains dark
in spite of all those shining stars."

جلال‌الدین محمد رومی

Preface

H.D. Greaves

Edward FitzGerald, renowned world-wide for his translation (he called it a 'transmogrification') of the *Rubáiyát of Omar Khayyám*, began his foray into the Persian language with *Salámán and Absál*, an allegory by the Sufi poet-theologian, Jámí.

Respected for his eloquence, as well as his study of the metaphysics of divine mercy, Jámí was born on 7 November 1414, and died on 9 November 1492 (the actual dates are suspect). Following the poem, you will find Edward FitzGerald's *Life of Jámí*. Further information may be found in libraries and on the internet—far too much information, certainly, than is necessary for this slender volume, which concerns itself only with FitzGerald's translation of Jámí's *Salámán and Absál*.

Introduced to Jámí's writings, and to this allegorical poem in particular, by his friend, E.B. Cowell, a young Oriental scholar (who later became Professor of Sanscrit at Cambridge), FitzGerald, a most unusual

i

nineteenth century Victorian gentleman, identified himself in some mystical way with ancient Persian language and thought. Here, in FitzGerald's words, is an excerpt from his letter to Cowell about the beginnings of the translation:

"My dear Cowell,

Two years ago, when we began (I for the first time) to read this Poem together, I wanted you to translate it, as something that should interest a few who are worth interesting. You, however, did not see the way clear then . . . So, continuing to like old Jámí more and more, I must try my hand upon him, and here is my reduced Version of a small Original. What scholarship it has is yours, my Master in Persian and so much beside; who are no further answerable for all than by well liking and wishing publish't what you may scarce have Leisure to find due fault with."

Whatever fine qualities Jámí's Persian possessed in the fifteenth century, FitzGerald's remarkable nineteenth century translation into English reflects the influences of his own time, which are powerfully Miltonic.

Consequently, in FitzGerald's words, his translation, "as something that should interest a few who are worth interesting," should perhaps be best read and enjoyed in the Miltonesque spirit of the nineteenth century.

Of course, if allegory is not to your taste, as it was famously not to the taste of J.R.R. Tolkien, this volume is not for you.

For the rest, those "few who are worth interesting," this romantic allegory of love, loss, wisdom, and destiny will, with only a little effort, transport you to a charming and exotic world far removed from our still young and already turbulent twenty-first century.

The Footnotes throughout the poem are by Edward FitzGerald.

Salámán and Absál

Prologue

O h Thou whose Memory quickens Lovers' Souls,
Lovers' Souls,
Whose Fount of Joy renews the Lover's
Tongue,
Thy Shadow falls across the World, and they
Bow down to it; and of the Rich in Beauty
Thou art the Riches that make Lovers mad.
Not till thy Secret Beauty through the Cheek
Of LAILA smite does she inflame MAJNÚN,[1]
And not until Thou have sugar'd SHÍRÍN's Lip
The Hearts of those Two Lovers fill with Blood.[2]
For Lov'd and Lover are not but by Thee,
Nor Beauty;—Mortal Beauty but the Veil
Thy Heavenly hides behind, and from itself
Feeds, and our Hearts yearn after as a Bride
That glances past us Veil'd—but ever so
As none the Beauty from the Veil may know.
How long wilt thou continue thus the World

---

[1] All well-known Types of Eastern Lovers, Shírín and her Suitors figure in Section xx.

[2] The Persian Mystics also represent the Deity Diceing with Human Destiny behind the Curtain.

To cozen with the Fantom of a Veil
From which Thou only peepest?—Time it is
To unfold thy perfect Beauty. I would be
Thy Lover, and Thine only—I, mine Eyes
Seal'd in the Light of Thee to all but Thee:
Yea, in the Revelation of Thyself
Self—Lost, and Conscience—quit of Good and
Evil.
Thou movest under all the Forms of Truth,
Under the Forms of all Created Things;
Look whence I will, still nothing I discern
But Thee in all the Universe, in which
Thyself Thou dost invest, and through the Eyes
Of Man, the subtle Censor[3] Scrutinize.
No Entrance finds—no Word of THIS and THAT;
Do Thou my separate and Derivéd Self
Make one with thy Essential! Leave me room,
On that Diván which leaves no Room for Two;[4]
Lest, like the Simple Kurd of whom they tell,

---

[3] 'The Appollonius of Keats's *Lamnia*.'

[4] This Súfi Identification with Deity (further illustrated in the Story of Section xix.) is shadowed in a Parable of Jeladdín, of which here in an outline. 'One knocked at the Belovéd's door; and a voice asked from within, "Who is there?" and he answered, "It is I," Then the Voice said, "This house will not hold Me and Thee." And the Door was not opened. Then went the Lover into the Desert, and fasted and prayed in Solitude. And after a Year he returned and knocked again at the Door. And again the Voice asked, "Who is there?" and he said, "It is Thyself!"—and the Door was opened to him.'

I grow perplext, Oh God! 'twixt 'I' and 'THOU;'
If *I*—this Dignity and Wisdom whence?
If *THOU*—then what this abject Impotence?

A Kurd perplext by Fortune's Frolics
Left his Desert for the City.
Sees a City full of Noise and
Clamour, agitated People,
Hither, Thither, Back and Forward
Running, some intent on Travel,
Others home again returning,
Right to Left, and Left to Right,
Life-disquiet everywhere!
Kurd, when he beholds the Turmoil,
Creeps aside, and, Travel-weary,
Fain would go to Sleep; "But," saith he,
"How shall I in all this Hubbub
"Know myself again on waking?"
So by way of Recognition
Ties a Pumpkin round his Foot,
And turns to Sleep. A Knave that heard him
Crept behind, and slily watching
Slips the Pumpkin off Sleeper's
Ancle, ties it round his own,
And so down to sleep beside him.
By and by the Kurd awaking
Looks directly for his Signal—

Sees it on another's Ancle—
Cries aloud, 'Oh, Good-for-Nothing
Rascal to perplex me so!
That by you I am bewilder'd,
If I—the Pumpkin why on *You*?
If *You*—then Where am *I*, and *WHO*?'

Oh God! this poor bewilder'd Kurd am I,
Than any Kurd more helpless!—Oh, do thou
Strike down a Ray of Light into my Darkness!
Turn by thy Grace, these Dregs into pure Wine,
To recreate the Spirits of the Good!
Or if not that, yet, as the little Cup
Whose Name I go by,[5] not unworthy found
I listen in the tavern of Sweet Songs,
And catch no Echo of their Harmony:
The Guests have drunk the Wine and are
departed,
Leaving their empty Bowls behind—not one
To carry on the Revel Cup in hand!
Up Jámí then! and whether Lees or Wine
To offer—boldly offer it in Thine.

---

[5] The Poet's name, Jámí, also signifying 'A Cup.' The Poet's Yúsuf and Zulaikha,' opens also with this Divine Wine, the favourite symbol of Háfiz and other Persian Mystics. *The Tavern* spoken of is The World.

2

And yet how long, Jámí, in this Old House
Stringing thy Pearls upon a Harp of Song?
Year after Year striking up some new Song,
The Breath of some Old Story?[6] Life is gone,
And yet the song is not the Last; my Soul
Is spent—and still a Story to be told!
And I, whose Back is crookéd as the Harp
I still keep tuning through the Night till Day!
That Harp untun'd by Time—the Harper's hand
Shaking with Age—how shall the Harper's
hand
Repair its cunning, and the sweet old Harp
Be modulated as of old? Methinks
'Tis time to break and cast it in the Fire;
Yea, sweet the Harp that can be sweet no more,
To cast it in the Fire—the vain old Harp
That can no more sound Sweetness to the Ear,
But burn'd may breathe sweet Attár to the Soul,
And comfort so the Faith and Intellect,
Now that the Body looks to Dissolution.
My Teeth fall out—my two Eyes see no more
Till by Feringhi Glasses[7] turn'd to Four;
Pain sits with me sitting behind my knees,

---

[6] Yúsuf and Zulaikha, Laila and Majnún, etc.

[7] First notice of Spectacles in Oriental Poetry, perhaps.

From which I hardly rise unhelpt of hand;
I bow down to my Root, and like a Child
Yearn, as is likely, to my Mother Earth,
With whom I soon shall cease to moan and
weep,
And on my Mother's Bosom fall asleep.
The House in Ruin, and its Music heard
No more within, nor at the Door of Speech,
Better in Silence and Oblivion
To fold me Head and Foot, remembering
What that BELOVED to the Master whisper'd:—
"No longer think of Rhyme, but think of Me!"—
Of WHOM?—of Him whose Palace THE SOUL is,
And Treasure-House—who notices and knows
Its Income and Out-going, and *then* comes
To fill it when the Stranger is departed.
Whose Shadow being KINGS—whose Attributes
The Type of Theirs—their Wrath and Favour
His
Lo! in the Celebration of His Glory.
The KING Himself comes on me unaware,
And suddenly arrests me for his own.
Wherefore once more I take—best quitted
else—
The Field of Verse, to Chaunt that double
Praise,

And in that Memory refresh my Soul
Until I grasp the Skirt of Living Presence.

One who travel'd in the Desert
Saw Majnún where he was sitting
All alone like a Magician
Tracing Letters in the Sand.
"Oh distracted Lover! writing
What the Sword-wind of the Desert
Undecyphers soon as written,
So that none who travels after
Shall be able to interpret!"—
Majnún answer'd, "I am writing
'Lailí'—were it only 'Lailí,'
Yet a BOOK of Love and Passion;
And, with but her Name to dote on,
Amorously I caress it
As it were Herself, and sip
Her Presence till I drink her Lip."

3

When Night had thus far brought me with my
Book,
In middle Thought Sleep robb'd me of myself;
And in a Dream Myself I seem'd to see,
Walking along a straight and even Road,
And clean as is the Soul of the Súfi;
A Road whose spotless Surface neither Breeze
Lifted in Dust, nor mix'd the Rain to Mire.
There I, methought, was pacing tranquilly,
When, on a sudden, the tumultuous Shout
Of Soldiers behind broke on mine Ear,
And took away my Wit and Strength for Fear.
I look'd about for Refuge, and Behold!
A Palace was before me; whither running
For Refuge from the coming Soldiery,
Suddenly from the Troop a Sháhzemán,[8]
By Name and Nature HASAN—on the Horse
Of Honour mounted—robed in Royal Robes,
And wearing a White Turban on his Head,
Turn'd his Rein tow'rd me, and with smiling
Lips

---

[8] 'Lord of the World, SOVEREIGN; HASAN, BEAUTIFUL, GOOD.'
HASAN Beg of Western Persia, famous for his Beauty, had helped
Jámí with Escort in a dangerous Pilgrimage. He died (as History and a
previous line in the Original tell) before Salámán was written, and was
succeeded by his Son Yácúb.

Open'd before my Eyes the Door of Peace.
Then, riding up to me, dismounted; kiss'd
My Hand, and did me Courtesy; and I,
How glad of his Protection, and the Grace
He gave it with!—Who then of gracious Speech
Many a Jewel utter'd; but of these
Not one that in my Ear till Morning hung.
When, waking on my Bed, my waking Wit
I question'd what the Vision meant, it answered;
"This Courtesy and Favour of the Shah
Foreshadows the fair Acceptance of thy Verse,
Which lose no moment pushing to Conclusion."
This hearing, I address'd me like a Pen
To steady Writing; for perchance, I thought,
From the same Fountain whence the Vision
grew
The Interpretation also may come True.

    Breathless ran a simple Rustic
    To a Cunning Man of Dreams;
    "Lo, this Morning I was dreaming—
    And, methought, in yon deserted
    Village wander'd—all about me
    Shatter'd Houses—and, Behold!
    Into one, methought, I went—and
    Search'd—and found a Hoard of Gold!"
    Quoth the Prophet in Derision,

جلال‌الدین محمد رومی

"Oh Thou Jewel of Creation,
Go and sole your Feet like Horse's,
And returning to your Village
Stamp and scratch with Hoof and Nail,
And give Earth so sound a Shaking,
She must hand you something up."
Went at once the unsuspecting
Countryman; with hearty Purpose
Set to work as he was told;
And, the very first Encounter,
Struck upon his Hoard of Gold!

Until Thou hast thy Purpose by the Hilt,
Catch at it boldly—or Thou never wilt.

4

THE STORY

A SHAH there was who ruled the Realm of Yún,[9]
And wore the Ring of Empire of Sikander;
And in his Reign A SAGE, who had the Tower
Of Wisdom of so strong Foundation built
That Wise Men from all Quarters of the World
To catch the Word of Wisdom from his Lip
Went in a Girdle round him.—Which THE SHAH
Observing, took him to his Secresy;
Stirr'd not a Step nor set Design afoot
Without that Sage's sanction; till, so counsel'd,
From Káf to Káf[10] reach'd his Dominion:
No Nation of the World or Nation's Chief
Who wore the Ring but under span of his
Bow'd down the Neck; then rising up in Peace
Under his Justice grew, and knew no Wrong,
And in their Strength was his Dominion Strong.

The SHAH that has not Wisdom in Himself,

---

[9] Or 'YAVAN,' Son of Japhet, from whom the Country was called 'YÚNAN,'—Ionia, meant by the Persians to express Greece generally. Sikander is, of course, Alexander the Great, of whose Ethics Jámí wrote, as Nizami of his Deeds.

[10] The Fabulous Mountain supposed by Asiatics to surround the World, binding the Horizon on all sides.

Nor has a Wise Man for his Counsellor,
The Wand of his Authority falls short,
And his Dominion crumbles at the Base.
For he, discerning not the Characters
Of Tyranny and Justice, confounds both,
Making the World a Desert, and the Fount
Of Justice a Seráb.[11] Well was it said,
"*Better just Káfir than Believing Tyrant.*"

> God said to the Prophet David,—
> "David, speak, and to the Challenge
> Answer of the Faith within Thee.
> Even Unbelieving Princess,
> Ill-reported if Unworthy,
> Yet, if They be Just and Righteous,
> Were their Worship of THE FIRE—
> Even These unto Themselves
> Reap glory and redress the World."

---

[11] Miráge; but, of two Foreign Words, why not the more original Persian?—identical with the Hebrew Sháráb, as in Isaiah xv., 7, 'The *Sháráb* (or *Miráge*) shall become a Lake;' —rather, and better, than our Version, 'The parched Ground shall become a Pool.' *See* Genenius.

5

One Night THE SHAH of Yúnan, as his wont,
Consider'd of his Power, and told his State,
How great it was, and how about him sat
The Robe of Honour of Prosperity;
Then found he nothing wanted to his Heart,
Unless a Son, who his Dominion
And Glory might inherit after him.
And then he turn'd him to THE SHAH, and said;
"Oh Thou, whose Wisdom is the Rule of
Kings—
(Glory to God who gave it!)—answer me;
Is any Blessing better than a Son?
Man's prime Desire; by which his Name and He
Shall live beyond Himself; by whom his Eyes
Shine living, and his Dust with Roses blows;
A Foot for Thee to stand on, he shall be
A Hand to stop thy Falling; in his Youth
Thou shalt be Young, and in his Strength be
Strong;
Sharp shall he be in Battle as a Sword,
A Cloud of Arrows on the Enemy's Head;
His Voice shall cheer his Friends to "Plight,
And turn the Foeman's Glory into Flight."
Thus much of a Good Son, whose wholesome
Growth

Approves the Root he grew from; but for one
Kneaded of Evil—Well, could one undo
His Generation, and as early pull
Him and his Vices from the String of Time.
Like Noah's, puff'd with Ignorance and Pride,
Who felt the Stab of "He IS NONE OF THINE!"
And perish'd in the Deluge.[12] And because
All are not Good, be slow to pray for One,
Whom having you may have to pray to lose.

Crazy for the Curse of Children,
Ran before the Sheikh a Fellow,
Crying out, "Oh hear and help me!
Pray to Allah from my Clay
To raise me up a fresh young Cypress,

---

[12] In the Kurán God engaged to save Noah and his Family—meaning
all who believed in the Warning. One of Noah's Sons (Canaan or Yam,
some think) would not believe. 'And the Ark swam with them between
waves like Mountains, and Noah called up to his Son, who was
separated from him, saying, "Embark with us, my Son, and stay not
with the Unbelievers." He answered, "I will get on a Mountain which
will secure me from the Water." Noah replied, "There is no security
this Day from the Decree of God, except for him on whom he shall
have Mercy." And a Wave passed between them, and he became one of
those who were drowned. And it was said, "Oh Earth, swallow up thy
waters, and thou, oh Heaven, withhold thy Rain!" and immediately the
Water abated and the Decree was fulfilled, and the Ark rested on the
Mountain Al Judi, and it was said, "Away with the ungodly People!"—
Noah called upon his Lord and said, "Oh Lord, verily my Son is of my
Family, and thy Promise is True; for Thou art of those who exercise
Judgment." God answered, "Oh Noah, verily he is not of thy Family;
this intercession of thine for him is not a righteous work." *Sale's
Kurán*, vol. ii, p.21

Who my Childless Eyes may lighten
With the Beauty of his Presence."
Said the Sheikh, "Be wise, and leave it
Wholly in the Hand of Allah,
Who, whatever we are after,
Understands our Business best."
But the Man persisted, saying,
"Sheikh, I languish in my Longing;
Help, and set my Prayer a-going!"
Then the Sheikh held up his Hand—
Pray'd—his Arrow flew to Heaven—
From the Hunting-ground of Darkness
Down a musky Fawn of China
Brought—a Boy—who, when the Tender
Shoot of Passion in him planted
Found sufficient Soil and Sap,
Took to Drinking with his Fellows;
From a Corner of the House-top
Ill affronts a Neighbour's Wife,
Draws his Dagger on the Husband,
Who complains before the Justice,
And the Father has to pay.
Day and Night the Youngster's Doings
Such—the Talk of all the City;
Nor Entreaty, Threat, or Counsel
Held him; till the Desperate Father

Once more to the Sheikh a-running,
Catches at his Garment, crying—
"Sheikh, my only Hope and Helper!
One more Prayer! that God who laid
Will take that Trouble from my Head!"
But the Sheikh replied: "Remember
How that very Day I warn'd you
Better not importune Allah;
Unto whom remains no other
Prayer, unless to pray for Pardon.
When from this World we are summon'd
On to bind the pack of Travel
Son or Daughter ill shall help us;
Slaves we are, and unencumber'd
Best may do the Master's mind;
And, whatever he may order,
Do it with a Will Resign'd."

6

When the Sharp-witted SAGE
Had heard these Sayings of THE SHAH, he said,
"Oh SHAH, who would not be the Slave of Lust
Must still endure the Sorrow of no Son.
—Lust that makes blind the Reason; Lust that makes
A Devil's self seem Angel to our Eyes;
A Cataract that, carrying havoc with it,
Confounds the prosperous House; a Road of Mire
Where whoso falls he rises not again;
A Wine of which whoever tastes shall see
Redemption's face no more—one little Sip
Of that delicious and unlawful Drink
Making crave much, and hanging round the Palate
Till it become a Ring to lead thee by[13]
(Putting the rope in a Vain Woman's hand),
Till thou thyself go down the Way of Nothing."

"For what is Woman? A Foolish, Faithless Thing—
To whom The Wise Self-subjected, himself

---

[13] *'Mihar'*—a Piece of Wood put through a Camel's Nose to guide him by.

Deep sinks beneath the Folly he sets up.
A very Káfir in Rapacity;
Clothe her a hundred Years in Gold and Jewel,
Her Garment with Brocade of Susa braided,
Her very Night-gear wrought in Cloth of Gold,
Dangle her Ears with Ruby and with Pearl,
Her House with Golden Vessels all a-blaze,
Her Tables loaded with the Fruit of Kings,
Ispahan Apples, Pomegranates of Yazd;
And, be she thirsty, from a Jewell'd Cup
Drinking the Water of the Well of Life—
One little twist of Temper,—all you've done
Goes all for Nothing. 'Torment of my Life!'
She cries, 'What have you ever done for Me!'—
Her Brow's white Tablet—Yes—'tis uninscrib'd
With any Letter of Fidelity;
Who ever read it there? Lo, in your Bosom
She lies for Years—you turn away a moment,
And she forgets you—worse, if as you turn
Her Eye should light on any Younger Lover."

  Once upon the Throne of Judgment,
    Telling one another Secrets,
  Sat SULAYMAN and BALKIS;[14]
    The Hearts of Both were turn'd to Truth,

---

[14] Solomon and the Queen of Sheba.

Unsullied by Deception.
First the King of Faith SULAYMAN
Spoke—"Though mine the Ring of Empire,
a Never any Day that passes
Darkens any one my Door-way
But into his Hand I look
And He who comes not empty-handed
Grows to Honour in mine Eyes."
After this BALKÍS a Secret
From her hidden Bosom utter'd,
Saying—"Never Night or Morning
Comely Youth before me passes
Whom I look not longing after;
Saying to myself, 'Oh were he
Comforting of my Sick Soul!—"

"If this, as wise Ferdúsi says, the Curse
Of Better Women, what should be the Worse?"

7

THE SAGE his Satire ended; and THE SHAH
With Magic-mighty WISDOM his pure WILL
Leaguing, its Self-fulfilment wrought from
Heaven.
And Lo! from Darkness came to Light A CHILD,
Of Carnal Composition Unattaint,—
A Rosebud blowing on the Royal Stem,—
A Perfume from the Realm of Wisdom wafted;
The Crowning Jewel of the Crown; a Star
Under whose Augury triumph'd the Throne.
For whose Auspicious Name they clove the
Words
"SALÁMAT"—Incolumity from Evil—
And "AUSEMÁN"—the Heav'n from which he
came
And hail'd him by the title of SALÁMÁN.
And whereas from no Mother Milk he drew,
They chose for him a Nurse—her name
ABSÁL—
Her Years not Twenty—from the Silver Line
Dividing the Musk-Harvest of her Hair
Down to her Foot that trampled Crowns of
Kings,
A Moon of Beauty Full; who thus elect

SALÁMÁN of Auspicious Augury
Should carry in the Garment of her Bounty,
Should feed Him with the Flowing of her
Breast.
As soon as she had opened Eyes on him
She closed those Eyes to all the World beside,
And her Soul crazed, a-doting on her Jewel,
Her Jewel in a Golden Cradle set;
Opening and shutting which her Day's Delight,
To gaze upon his Heart-inflaming Cheek,
Upon the Darling whom, could she, she would
Have cradled as the Baby of her Eye.[15]
In Rose and Musk she wash'd him—to his Lips
Press'd the pure Sugar from the Honeycomb;
And when, Day over, she withdrew her Milk,
She made, and having laid him in, his Bed,
Burn'd all Night like a Taper o'er his Head.

Then still as Morning came, and as he grew,
She dress'd him like a Little Idol up;
On with his Robe—with fresh Collyrium Dew
Touch'd his Narcissus Eyes—the Musky Locks
Divided from his Forehead—and embraced
With Gold and Ruby Girdle his fine Waist.—

---

[15]THE EYE'S BABY: literally, MARDUMAK—the MANNIKIN, Or PUPIL, of the Eye, corresponding to the Image so frequently used by our old Poets.

So rear'd she him till full Fourteen his Years,
Fourteen-day full the Beauty of his Face,
That rode high in a Hundred Thousand Hearts;
Yea, when SALÁMÁN was but Half-lance high,
Lance-like he struck a wound in every One,
And burn'd and shook down Splendour like a
Sun.

8

Soon as the Lord of Heav'n had sprung his
Horse
Over the Horizon into the Blue Field,
SALÁMÁN rose drunk with the Wine of Sleep,
And set himself a-stirrup for the Field;
He and a Troop of Princes—Kings in Blood,
Kings too in the Kingdom-troubling Tribe of
Beauty,
All Young in Years and Courage,[16] Bat in hand
Gallop'd a-field, toss'd down the Golden Ball
And chased, so many Crescent Moons a Full;
And, all alike Intent upon the Game,
SALÁMÁN still would carry from them all
The Prize, and shouting "Hál!" drive Home the
Ball.[17]
This done, SALÁMÁN bent him as a Bow
To Shooting—from the Marksmen of the World
Call'd for an unstrung Bow—himself the Cord
Fitted unhelpt,[18] and nimbly with his hand

---

[16] The same Persian word serving for both.
[17] THE BALL.—the Game of CHÚGÁN, for Centuries the Royal Game of Persia, and adopted (Ouseley thinks) under varying modifications of Name and Practice by other Nations, was played by Horsemen, who, suitably habited, and armed with semicircular-headed Bats or Sticks so short the Player must stoop below the Saddle-bow to strike, strove to drive a Ball through a Goal of upright Pillars.

[18] FITTING THE CORD.—bows being so gradually stiffened, to the Age

Twanging made cry, and drew it to his Ear:
Then, fixing the Three-feather'd Fowl,
discharged.
No point in Heaven's Azure but his Arrow
Hit; nay, but Heaven were made of Adamant,
Would overtake the Horizon as it roll'd;
And, whether aiming at the Fawn a-foot,
Or Bird on wing, his Arrow went away
Straight—like the Soul that cannot go astray.

When Night came, that releases Man from Toil,
He play'd the Chess of Social Intercourse;
Prepared his Banquet Hall like Paradise,
Summon'd his Houri-faced Musicians,
And, when his Brain grew warm with Wine, the
Veil
Flung off him of Reserve. Now Lip to Lip
Concerting with the Singer he would breathe
Like a Messias Life into the Dead;
Now made of the Melodious-moving Pipe
A Sugar-cane between his Lips that ran
Men's Ears with Sweetness: Taking up a Harp,

---

and Strength of the Archer, as at last to need five Hundredweight of
Pressure to bend, says an old Translation of Chardin, who describes all
the Process up to bringing up the String to the Ear, "as if to hang it
there" before Shooting. Then the First Trial was, who could shoot
highest; then, the Mark, etc.

Between its dry String and his Finger fresh
Struck Fire; or lifting in his arms a Lute
As if a little Child for Chastisement,
Pinching its Ear such Cries of Sorrow wrung
As drew Blood to the Eyes of Older Men.
Now sang He like the Nightingale alone,
Now set together Voice and Instrument;
And thus with his Associates Night he spent.

His Soul rejoiced in Knowledge of all kinds;
The fine Edge of his Wit would split a Hair,
And in the Noose of Apprehension catch
A Meaning ere articulate in Word;
His Verse was like the PLEIADS;[19] his Discourse
The MOURNERS OF THE BIER; his Penmanship,
(Tablet and running Reed his Worshippers,)
Fine on the Lip of Youth as the First Hair,
Drove Penmen, as that Lovers, to Despair.

His Bounty was as Ocean's—nay, the Sea's
Self but the Foam of his Munificence,
For it threw up the Shell, but he the Pearl;

---

[19] THE PLEIADS.—i.e. compactly strung, as opposed to Discursive
Rhetoric, which is compared to the scattered Stars of THE BIER AND ITS
MOURNERS, or what we call THE GREAT BEAR. This contrast is
otherwise prettily applied in the Anvari Soheili—"When one grows
poor, his Friends, heretofore compact as THE PLEIADS, disperse wide
asunder as THE MOURNERS."

جلال‌الدین محمد رومی

He was a Cloud that rain'd upon the World
Dirhems for Drops; the Banquet of whose
Bounty
Left Hátim's[20] Churlish in Comparison—

---

[20] The Persian Type of Liberality, infinitely celebrated.

9

Suddenly that Sweet Minister of mine
Rebuked me angrily; "What Folly, Jámí,
Wearing that indefatigable Pen
In celebration of an Alien SHAH
Whose Throne, not grounded in the Eternal
World,
YESTERDAY was, TO-DAY is not!"[21] "I answer'd;
Oh Fount of Light!—under an Alien Name
I shadow One upon whose Head the Crown
Both WAS and IS TO-DAY; to whose Firmán
The Seven Kingdoms of the World are subject,
And the Seas Seven but droppings of his
Largess.
Good luck to him who under other Name
Taught us to veil the Praises of a Power
To which the Initiate scarce find open Door."

Sat a Lover solitary
Self-discoursing in a Corner,
Passionate and ever-changing
Invocation pouring out;
Sometimes Sun and Moon; and sometimes
Under Hyacinth half-hidden

---

[21] AN ALIEN SHAH.—the Hero of the Story being of YÚNAN—IONIA, or
GREECE generally, (the Persian Geography not being very precise,)—
and so not of THE FAITH.

Roses; or the lofty Cypress,
And the little Weed below.
Nightingaling thus a Noodle
Heard him, and, completely puzzled,
"What!" quoth he, "And you, a Lover,
Raving not about your Mistress,
But about the Moon and Roses!"
Answer'd he; "Oh thou that aimest
Wide of Love, and Lover's Language
Wholly misinterpreting;
Sun and Moon are but my Lady's
Self, as any Lover knows;
Hyacinth I said, and meant her
a Hair—her Cheek was in the Rose—
And I myself the wretched Weed
That in her Cypress Shadow grows."

10

Now was SALÁMÁN in his Prime of Growth,
His Cypress Stature risen to high Top,
And the new-blooming Garden of his Beauty
Began to bear; and Absál long'd to gather;
But the Fruit grew upon too high a Bough,
To which the Noose of her Desire was short.
She too rejoiced in Beauty of her own
No whit behind SALÁMÁN, whom she now
Began enticing with her Sorcery.
Now from her Hair would twine a musky Chain,
To bind his Heart—now twist it into Curls
Nestling innumerable Temptations;
Doubled the Darkness of her Eyes with Surma
To make him lose his way, and over them
Adorn'd the Bows[22] that were to shoot him
then;
Now to the Rose-leaf of her Cheek would add
Fresh Rose, and then a Grain of Musk[23] lay
there,
The Bird of the Belovéd Heart to snare.
Now with a Laugh would break the Ruby Seal

---

[22] ADORNING THE BOWS: with dark Indigo Paint, as the Archery Bow
with a thin Papyrus-like Bark.

[23] A GRAIN OF MUSK.—a 'PATCH,' sc.—"Noir comme le Musc."—De
Sacy.

That lockt up Pearl; or busied in the Room
Would smite her Hand perhaps—on that pretence
To lift and show the Silver in her Sleeve;
Or hastily rising clash her Golden Anclets
To draw the Crowned Head under her Feet.
Thus by innumerable Bridal wiles
She went about soliciting his Eyes,
Which she would scarce let lose her for a Moment;
For well she knew that mainly by THE Eye
Love makes his Sign, and by no other Road
Enters and takes possession of the Heart.

Burning with Desire ZULAIKHA
Built a Chamber, Wall and Ceiling
Blank as an untarnisht Mirror,
Spotless as the Heart of Yúsuf.
Then she made a cunning Painter
Multiply her Image round it;
Not an Inch of Wall but echoed
With the Reflex of her Beauty.
Then amid them all in all her
Glory sat she down, and sent for
Yúsuf—she began a Tale
Of Love—and Lifted up her Veil.
From her Look he turn'd, but turning

Wheresoever, ever saw her
Looking, looking at him still.
Then Desire arose within him—
He was almost yielding—almost
Laying Honey on her Lip—
When a Signal out of Darkness
Spoke to him—and he withdrew
His Hand, and dropt the Skirt of Fortune.

11

Thus day by day did ABSÁL tempt SALÁMÁN,
And by and bye her Wiles began to work.
Her Eyes Narcissus stole his Sleep—their
Lashes
Pierc'd to his Heart—out from her Locks a
Snake
Bit him—and bitter, bitter on his Tongue
Became the Memory of her honey Lip.
He saw the Ringlet restless on her Cheek,

And he too quiver'd with Desire; his Tears
Burn'd Crimson from her Cheek, whose musky
spot
Infected all his soul with Melancholy.
Love drew him from behind the Veil, where yet
Withheld him better Resolution—
"Oh, should the Food I long for, tasted, turn
Unwholesome, and if all my Life to come
Should sicken from one momentary Sweet!"

On the Sea-shore sat a Raven,
Blind, and from the bitter Cistern
Forc'd his only Drink to draw.
Suddenly the Pelican
Flying over Fortune's Shadow
Cast upon his Head,[24] and calling—

"Come, poor Son of Salt, and taste of
Sweet, sweet Water from my Maw."
Said the Raven, "If I taste it
Once, the Salt I have to live on
May for ever turn to Loathing;
And I sit a Bird accurst
Upon the Shore to die of Thirst."

---

[24] FORTUNE'S SHADOW—alluding to the Phœnix, the Shadow of whose
wings foretold a Crown upon the Head it passed over.

12

Now when SALÁMÁN'S Heart turn'd to ABSÁL,
Her Star was happy in the Heavens—Old Love
Put forth afresh—Desire doubled his Bond:
And of the running Time she watch'd an Hour
To creep into the Mansion of her Moon
And satiate her soul upon his Lips.
And the Hour came; she stole into his Chamber
Ran up to him, Life's offer in her Hand—
And, falling like a Shadow at his Feet,
She laid her Face beneath. SALÁMÁN then
With all the Courtesies of Princely Grace
Put forth his Hand—he rais'd her in his Arms
He held her trembling there—and from that
Fount
Drew first Desire; then Deeper from her Lips,
That, yielding, mutually drew from his
A Wine that ever drawn from never fail'd—

So through the Day—so through another
still—
The Day became a Seventh—the Seventh a
Moon—
The Moon a Year—while they rejoiced
together,
Thinking their Pleasure never was to end.

But rolling Heaven whisper'd from his Ambush,
"So in my License is it not set down.
Ah for the sweet Societies I make
At Morning and before the Nightfall break;
Ah for the Bliss that with the Setting Sun
I mix, and, with his Rising, all is done!"

Into Bagdad came a hungry
Arab—after many days of waiting
In to the Khalífah's Supper
Push'd, and got before a Pasty
Luscious as the Lip of Beauty,
Or the Tongue of Eloquence.
Soon as seen, Indecent Hunger
Seizes up and swallows down;
Then his mouth undaunted wiping—
"Oh Khalífah, hear me Swear,
Not of any other Pasty
Than of Thine to sup or dine."
The Khalífah laugh'd and answer'd;
"Fool! who thinkest to determine
What is in the Hands of Fate—
Take and thrust him from the Gate!"

13

While a Full Year was counted by the Moon,
SALÁMÁN and ABSÁL rejoiced together,
And for so long he stood not in the face
Of SAGE or SHAH, and their bereavéd Hearts
Were torn in twain with the Desire of Him.
They question'd those about him, and from them
Heard something; then Himself in Presence summon'd,
And, subtly sifting on all sides, so plied
Interrogation till it hit the Mark,
And all the Truth was told. Then SAGE and SHAH
Struck out with Hand and Foot in his Redress.
And First with REASON, which is also Best;
REASON that rights the Retrograde—completes
The Imperfection—REASON that unties the Knot:
For REASON is the Fountain from of old
From which the Prophets drew, and none beside.
Who boasts of other Inspiration lies—
There are no other Prophets than THE WISE.

14

First spoke THE SHAH;—"SALÁMÁN, Oh my Soul,
Oh Taper of the Banquet of my House,
Light of the Eyes of my Prosperity,
And making bloom the Court of Hope with
Rose;
Years Rose-bud-like my own Blood I devour'd
Till in my hand I carried thee, my Rose;
Oh do not tear my Garment from my Hand,
Nor wound thy Father with a Dagger Thorn.
Years for thy sake the Crown has worn my
Brow,
And Years my Foot been growing to the
Throne
Only for Thee—Oh spurn them not with Thine;
Oh turn thy Face from Dalliance unwise,
Lay not thy Heart's hand on a Minion!
For what thy Proper Pastime? Is it not
To mount and manage RAKHSH[25] along the
Field;
Not, with no stouter weapon than a Love-lock,
Idly reclining on a Silver Breast.
Go, fly thine Arrow at the Antelope
And Lion—let not me my Lion see

---

[25]. RAKHSH—"LIGHTNING." The name of RUSTAM'S famous Horse in the SHAH-NAMEH.

Slain by the Arrow eyes of a Ghazal.
Go, flash thy Steel among the Ranks of Men,
And smite the Warriors' Necks; not, flying them,
Lay down thine own beneath a Woman's Foot.
Leave off such doing in the Name of God,
"Nor bring thy Father weeping to the Ground;
Years have I held myself aloft, and all
For Thee—Oh Shame if thou prepare my Fall!"

When before SHIRÚEH's Feet
Drencht in Blood fell KAI KHUSRAU,[26]
He declared this Parable—
"Wretch!—There was a Branch that, waxing
Wanton o'er the Root he drank from,
At a Draught the Living Water
Drain'd wherewith Himself to crown;
Died the Root—and with it died
The Branch—and barren was brought
down!"

---

[26] KHUSRAU PARVÍZ (Chosroc The Victorious), Son of NOSHÍRAVAN
The Great; slain, after Thirty Years of Prosperous Reign, by his Son,
SHIRÚEH, who, according to some, was in Love with his Father's
Mistress, SHÍRÍN. One of the most dramatic Tragedies in Persian
History.

15

SALÁMÁN heard—the Sea of his Soul was
mov'd,
And bubbled up with Jewels, and he said;
"Oh SHAH, I am the Slave of thy Desire,
Dust of thy Throne ascending Foot am I;
Whatever thou Desirest I would do,
But sicken of my own Incompetence;
Not in the Hand of my infirmer Will
To carry into Deed mine own Desire.
Time upon Time I torture mine own Soul,
Devising liberation from the Snare
I languish in. But when upon that Moon
I *think*, my Soul relapses—and when *look*—
I leave both Worlds behind to follow her!"

16

THE SHAH ceased Counsel, and THE SAGE
began.
"Oh Thou new Vintage of a Garden old,
Last Blazon of the Pen of 'LET THERE BE,'[27]
Who read'st the SEVEN AND FOUR:[28] interpretest
The writing on the Leaves of Night and Day—
Archetype of the Assembly of the World,
Who hold'st the Key of Adam's Treasury—
(Know thine own Dignity and slight it not,
For Thou art Greater yet than all I tell)—
The Mighty Hand that mix'd thy Dust inscribed
The Character of Wisdom on thy Heart;
Oh Cleanse thy Bosom of Material Form,
And turn the Mirror of the Soul to SPIRIT,
Until it be with SPIRIT all possest,
Drown'd in the Light of Intellectual Truth.
Oh veil thine Eyes from Mortal Paramour,
And follow not her Step!—For what is She?—
What is She but a Vice and a Reproach,
Her very Garment-hem Pollution!

---

[27] The Pen of "KÛN"—"Esto!"—The famous Passage of Creation
stolen from Genesis by the Kurán.

[28] SEVEN AND FOUR: Planets?—adding Sun, Moon, and the Nodal
Dragon's Head and Tail; according to the Sanscrit Astronomy adopted
by Persia. I [FitzGerald] have proposed "The Planets" for those
mysterious "SEVEN AND FOUR." But there is a large Choice, especially
for the ever-mystical "SEVEN."

For such Pollution madden not thine Eyes,
Waste not thy Body's Strength, nor taint thy
Soul,
Nor set the Body and the Soul in Strife!
Supreme is thine Original Degree,
Thy Star upon the Top of Heaven; but Lust
Will fling it down even unto the Dust!"

Quoth a Muezzin unto Crested
Chanticleer—"Oh Voice of Morning,
Not a Sage of all the Sages
Prophesies of Dawn, or startles
At the wing of Time, like Thee.
One so wise methinks were fitter
Perching on the Beams of Heaven,
Than with these poor Hens about him,
Raking in a Heap of Dung."
"And," replied the Cock, "in Heaven
Once I was; but by my Evil
Lust am fallen down to raking
With my wretched Hens about me
On the Dunghill. Otherwise
I were even now in Eden
With the Bird of Paradise."

17

When from THE SAGE these words SALÁMÁN heard,
The breath of Wisdom round his Palate blew;
He said—"Oh Darling of the Soul of Plato,
To whom a hundred Aristotles bow;
Oh Thou that an Eleventh to the Ten
Original INTELLIGENCES addest,[29]—
I lay my Face before Thee in the Dust,
The humblest Scholar of thy Court am I;
Whose every word I find a Well of Wisdom,
And hasten to imbibe it in my Soul.
But clear unto thy clearest Eye it is,
That Choice is not within Oneself—To Do,
Not in THE WILL, but in THE POWER, to Do.
From that which I originally am
How shall I swerve? or how put forth a Sign
Beyond the Power that is by Nature Mine?"

---

[29] This passage finds its explanation in the last Section.

18

Unto the Soul that is confused by Love
Comes Sorrow after Sorrow—most of all
To Love whose only Friendship is Reproof,
And overmuch of Counsel—whereby Love
Grows stubborn, and increases the Disease.
Love unreproved is a delicious food;
Reproved, is Feeding on one's own Heart's
Blood.
SALÁMÁN heard; his Soul came to his Lips;
Reproaches struck not ABSÁL out of him,
But drove Confusion in; bitter became
The Drinking of the sweet Draught of Delight,
And waned the Splendour of his Moon of
Beauty.
His Breath was Indignation, and his Heart
Bled from the Arrow, and his Anguish grew
How bear it?—Able to endure one wound,
From Wound on Wound no remedy but Flight;
Day after Day, Design upon Design,
He turn'd the Matter over in his Heart,
And, after all, no Remedy but Flight.
Resolv'd on that, he victuall'd and equipp'd
A Camel, and one Night he led it forth,
And mounted—he and ABSÁL at his side,
The fair SALÁMÁN and ABSÁL the Fair,

Together on one Camel side by side,
Twin Kernels in a single Almond packt.
And True Love murmurs not, however small
His Chamber—nay, the straitest best of all.

When the Moon of Canaan Yúsuf
Darken'd in the Prison of Ægypt,
Night by Night ZULAIKHA went
To see Him—for her Heart was broken.
Then to her said One who never
Yet had tasted of Love's Garden:
"Leavest thou thy Palace-Chamber
For the Felon's narrow Cell?"
Answer'd She, "Without my Lover,
Were my Chamber Heaven's Horizon,
It were closer than an Ant's eye;
And the Ant's eye wider-were
Than Heaven, my Lover with me there!"

19

Six days SALÁMÁN on the Camel rode,
And then Remembrance of foregone Reproach
Abode not by him; and upon the Seventh
He halted on the Seashore, and beheld
An Ocean boundless as the Heaven above,
That, reaching its Circumference from Káf
To Káf, down to the Back of GAU and MAHI[30]
Descended, and its Stars were Creatures' Eyes.
The Face of it was as it were a Range
Of moving Mountains; or as endless Hosts
Of Camels trooping from all Quarters up,
Furious, with the Foam upon their Lips.
In it innumerable glittering Fish
Like Jewels polish-sharp, to the sharp Eye
But for an Instant visible, glancing through
As Silver Scissors slice a blue Brocade;
Though were the Dragon from its Hollow
roused,
THE DRAGON of the Stars[31] would stare Aghast.

---

[30] GAU AND MAHI.—The Bull and Fish—the lowest Substantial Base of Earth. "He first made the Mountains; then cleared the Face of Earth from Sea; then fixed it fast on Gau; Gau on Mahi; and Mahi on Air; and Air on what? on NOTHING; Nothing upon Nothing, all is Nothing—Enough." Attar quoted in De Sacy's PENDNAMAH, XXXV.

[31] The Sidereal Dragon, whose Head, according to the Pauránic (or Poetic) Astronomers of the East, devoured the Sun and Moon in Eclipse. "But WE know," said Ramachandra to Sir W. Jones, "that the

SALÁMÁN eyes the Sea, and cast about
To cross it—and forthwith upon the Shore
Devis'd a Shallop like a Crescent Moon,
Wherein that Sun and Moon in happy Hour
Enter'd as into some Celestial Sign;
That, figured like a Bow, but Arrow-like
In Flight, was feathered with a little Sail,
And, pitcht upon the Water like a Duck,
So with her Bosom sped to her Desire.

When they had sailed their Vessel for a Moon,
And marred their Beauty with the wind o' the
Sea,
Suddenly in mid Sea revealed itself
An Isle, beyond Description beautiful;
An Isle that all was Garden; not a Bird
Of Note or Plume in all the World but there;
There as in Bridal Retinue arrayed
The Pheasant in his Crown, the Dove in her
Collar;
And those who tuned their Bills among the
Trees
That Arm in Arm from Fingers paralyzed
With any Breath of Air Fruit moist and dry
Down scattered in Profusion to their Feet,

---

supposed Head and Tail of the Dragon mean only the NODES, or Points
formed by Intersections of the Ecliptic and the Moon's Orbit."

Where Fountains of Sweet Water ran, and
round
Sunshine and Shadow chequer-chased the
Ground.
Here Iram Garden seem'd in Secresy
Blowing the Rosebud of its Revelation;
Or Paradise, forgetful of the Day
Of Audit, lifted from her Face the Veil.
SALÁMÁN saw the Isle, and thought no more
Or Further—there with ABSÁL, he sat down,
ABSÁL and He together side by side
Rejoicing like the Lily and the Rose,
Together like the Body and the Soul.
Under its Trees in one another's Arms
They slept—they drank its Fountains hand in
hand—
Sought Sugar with the Parrot—or in Sport
Paraded with the Peacock—raced the
Partridge
Or fell a-talking with the Nightingale.
There was the Rose without a Thorn, and there
The Treasure and no Serpent to beware—
What sweeter than your Mistress at your side
In such a Solitude, and none to Chide!

   Whisper'd one to WÁMIK—"Oh Thou
   Victim of the Wound of AZRA,

What is it that like a Shadow
Movest thou about in Silence
Meditating Night and Day?"
WÁMIK answer'd, "Even this—
To fly with AZRA to the Desert;
There by so remote a Fountain
That which e'er way one travell'd
League on League, one yet should never,
Never meet the Face of Man—
There to pitch my Tent—for ever
There to gaze on my Belovéd;
Gaze, till Gazing out of Gazing
Grew to BEING Her I gaze on,
SHE and I no more, but in one
Undivided Being blended.
All that is not ONE must ever
Suffer with the Wound of Absence;
And whoever in Love's City
Enters, finds but Room for ONE,
And but in ONENESS Union."

20

When by and bye THE SHAH was made aware
Of that Soul-wasting absence of his Son,
He reach'd a Cry to Heav'n—his Eye-lashes
Wept Blood—Search everywhere he set a-foot,
But none could tell the hidden Mystery.
Then bade he bring a Mirror that he had,
A Mirror, like the Bosom of the Wise,
Reflecting all the World,[32] and lifting up
The Veil from all its Secrets, Good and Evil.
That Mirror bade he bring, and, in its Face
Looking, beheld the Face of his Desire.
He saw those Lovers in the Solitude,
Turn'd from the World, and all its Ways, and
People,
And looking only in each other's Eyes,
And never finding any Sorrow there.
THE SHAH beheld them as they were, and Pity
Fell on his Eyes, and he reproach'd them not;
And, gathering all their Life into his hand,

---

[32] A MIRROR.—mythically attributed by the East—and in some wild
Western Avatar—to this Shah's Predecessor, Alexander the Great.
Perhaps, the Concave Mirror upon the Alexandrian Pharos, which by
Night projected such a fiery Eye over the Deep as not only was fabled
to exchange Glances with that on the Rhodian Colossus, and in Oriental
Imagination and Language to penetrate "THE WORLD," but by Day to
Reflect it to him who looked therein with Eyes to see. Our Reflecting
Telescope is going some way to realize the Alexandrian Fable.

Not a Thread lost, disposed in Order all.
Oh for the Noble Nature, and Clear Heart,
That, seeing Two who draw one Breath,
together
Drinking the Cup of Happiness and Tears
Unshatter'd by the Stone of Separation,
Is loath their sweet Communion to destroy,
Or cast a Tangle in the Skein of Joy.

The Arrows that assail the Lords of Sorrow
Come from the Hand of Retribution.
Do Well, that in thy Turn Well may betide Thee;
And turn from Ill, that Ill may turn beside Thee.

FIRHÁD, Moulder of the Mountain,
Love-distracted look'd to SHÍRÍN,
And SHÍRÍN the Sculptor's Passion
Saw, and turn'd her Heart to Him.

Then the Fire of Jealous Frenzy
Caught and carried up the Harvest
Of the Might of KAI KHUSRAU.

Plotting with that ancient Hag
Of Fate, the Sculptor's Cup he poison'd,
And remain'd the Lord of Love.

So—But Fate that Fate avenges
Arms SHIRÚE with the Dagger,
And at once from SHÍRÍN tore him,

Hurl'd him from the Throne of Glory.[33]

---

[33].HURL'D HIM, ETC.—One Story is that Khusrau had promised if Firhád cut through a Mountain, and brought a Stream through, Shírín should be his. Firhád was on the point of achieving his Work, when Khusrau sent an old Woman (here, perhaps, purposely confounded with Fate) to tell him Shírín was dead; whereon Firhád threw himself headlong from the Rock

21

But as the days went on, and still The Shah
Beheld Salámán how sunk in Absál,
And yet no Hand of better Effort lifted;
But still the Crown that shall adorn his Head,
And still the Throne that waited for his Foot,
Trampled from Memory by a Base Desire,
Of which the Soul was still Unsatisfied—
Then from the Sorrow of The Shah fell Fire;
To Gracelessness ungracious he became,
And, quite to shatter his rebellious Lust,
Upon Salámán all his Will discharged.[34]
And Lo! Salámán to his Mistress turn'd,
But could not reach her—looked and looked
again,
And palpitated toward her—but in Vain!
Oh Misery! what to the Bankrupt worse
Than Gold he cannot reach! To one athirst
Than Fountain to the Eye and Lip forbid!—
Or than Heaven opened to the Eyes in Hell!—
Yet, when Salámán's Anguish was extreme,
The Door of Mercy open'd in his Face;
He saw and knew his Father's Hand outstretcht
To lift him from Perdition—timidly,

---

[34] WILL DISCHARGED.—He Mesmerizes Him!—See also further on this Power of the Will in Sections XXIII. and XXVI.

Timidly tow'rd his Father's Face his own
He lifted, Pardon-pleading, Crime-confest,
As the stray Bird one day will find her Nest.

> A Disciple asked a Master,
> "By what Token should a Father
> Vouch for his reputed Son?"
> Said the Master, "By the Stripling,
> Howsoever Late or Early,
> Like to the reputed Father
> Growing—whether Wise or Foolish."

> "Lo the disregarded Darnel
> With itself adorns the Wheat-field,
> And for all the Early Season
> Satisfies the Farmer's Eye;
> But come once the Hour of Harvest,
> And another Grain shall answer,
> 'Darnel and no Wheat, am I.'"

22

When The Shah saw Salámán's face again,
And breath'd the Breath of Reconciliation,
He laid the Hand of Love upon his Shoulder,
The Kiss of Welcome on his Cheek, and said,
"Oh Thou, who lost, Love's Banquet lost its
Salt,
And Mankind's Eye its Pupil!—Thy Return
Is as another Sun to Heaven; a new
Rose blooming in the Garden of the Soul.
Arise, Oh Moon of Majesty unwaned!
The Court of the Horizon is thy Court,
Thy Kingdom is the Kingdom of the World!—
Lo! Throne and Crown await Thee—Throne and
Crown
Without thy Impress but uncurrent Gold,
Not to be stamp'd by one not Worthy Them;
Behold! The Rebel's Face is at thy Door;
Let him not triumph—let the Wicked dread
The Throne under thy Feet, the Crown upon thy
Head.
Oh Spurn them not behind Thee! Oh my Son,
Wipe Thou the Woman's Henna from thy Hand:
Withdraw Thee from the Minion[35] who from

---

[35] THE MINION.—"Shah" and "Sháhid" (Mistress)—a sort of Punning the Persian Poets are fond of.

Thee
Dominion draws; the Time is come to choose,
Thy Mistress or the World to hold or lose."

23

Four are the Signs of Kingly Aptitude;
Wise Head—clean Heart—strong Arm—and
open Hand.
Wise is He not—Continent cannot be—
Who binds himself to an unworthy Lust;
Nor Valiant, who submits to a weak Woman;
Nor Liberal, who cannot draw his Hand
From that in which so basely he is busied.
And of these Four who misses All or One
Is not the Bridegroom of Dominion.

Ah the poor Lover!—In the changing Hands
Of Day and Night no wretcheder than He!
No Arrow from the Bow of Evil Fate
But reaches him—one Dagger at his Throat,
Another comes to wound him from behind.
Wounded by Love—then wounded by reproof
Of Loving—and, scarce staunch't the Blood of
Shame
By flying from his Love—then, worst of all,
Love's back-blow of Revenge for having fled!
SALÁMÁN heard—he rent the Robe of Peace
He came to Loathe his Life, and long for Death,
(For better Death itself than Life in Death)
He turn's his face with ABSÁL to the Desert—
Enter'd the deadly Plain; Branch upon Branch

Cut down, and gather'd in a lofty Pile,
And fired. They look'd upon the Flames, those
Two—
They look'd, and they rejoiced; and hand in
hand
They sprang into the Fire. THE SHAH who saw,
In secret all had order'd; and the Flame,
Directed by his Self-fulfilling WILL,
Devouring utterly ABSÁL, pass'd by
SALÁMÁN harmless—the pure Gold return'd
Entire, but all the baser Metal burn'd.

24

Heaven's Dome is but a wondrous House of
Sorrow,
And Happiness therein a lying Fable.
When first they mix'd the Clay of Man, and
cloth'd
His Spirit in the Robe of Perfect Beauty,
For Forty Mornings did an Evil Cloud
Rain Sorrows over him from Head to Foot;
And when the Forty Mornings pass'd to Night,
Then came one Morning-shower—one
Morning-Shower
Of Joy—to Forty of the Rain of Sorrow!—
And though the better Fortune came at last
To seal the Work, yet every Wise Man knows
Such Consummation never can be here!
SALÁMÁN fired the Pile; and in the Flame
That, passing him, consumed ABSÁL like Straw,
Died his Divided Self, and there survived
His individual; and, like a Body
From which the Soul is parted, all alone.
Then rose his Cry to Heaven—his Eye lashes
Dropt Blood—his Sighs stood like a Smoke in
Heaven,
And Morning rent her Garment at his Anguish.[36]

He tore his Bosom with his Nails—he smote
Stone on his Bosom—looking then on hands
No longer lockt in hers, and lost their Jewel,
He tore them with his Teeth. And when came
Night,
He hid him in some Corner of the House,
And communed with the Phantom of his Love.
"Oh Thou whose Presence so long sooth'd my
Soul,
Now burnt with thy Remembrance! Oh so long
The Light that fed these Eyes now dark with
Tears!
Oh Long, Long home of Love now lost for Ever!
We were Together—that was all Enough—
We two rejoicing in each other's Eyes,
Infinitely rejoicing—all the World
Nothing to Us, nor We to All the World—
No Road to Reach us, nor an Eye to watch—
All Day we whisper'd in each other's Ears,
All Night we slept in one another's Arms—
All seem'd to our Desire, as if the Wand
Of unjust Fortune were for once too short.
Oh would to God that when I lit the Pyre
The Flame had left Thee Living and me Dead,

---

[36] ANGUISH.—"When the Cloud of Spring beheld the Evil Disposition
of Time,"Its Weeping fell upon the Jessamine and Hyacinth and Wild
Rose."—HAFIZ.

Not Living worse than Dead, depriv'd of Thee!
Oh were I but with Thee!—at any Cost
Stript of this terrible self Solitude!
Oh but with Thee Annihilation—lost,
Or in Eternal Intercourse renew'd!"

Slumber-drunk an Arab in the
Desert off his Camel tumbled,
Who the lighter of her Burden
Ran upon her road rejoicing.
When the Arab woke at morning,
Rubb'd his Eyes and look'd about him—
"Oh my Camel! Oh my Camel!"
Quoth he, "Camel of my Soul!—
That Lost with Her I lost might be,
"Or found, She might be found with Me!"

25

When in this Plight THE SHAH SALÁMÁN saw,
His Soul was struck with Anguish, and the Vein
Of Life within was strangled—what to do
He knew not. Then he turned him to THE SAGE—
"Oh Altar of the World, to whom Mankind
Directs the Face of Prayer in Weal or Woe,
Nothing but Wisdom can untie the Knot;
And art not Thou the Wisdom of the World,
The Master Key of all its Difficulties?
ABSÁL is perisht; and, because of Her,
SALÁMÁN dedicates his Life to Sorrow;
I cannot bring back Her, nor comfort Him.
Lo, I have said! My Sorrow is before Thee;
From thy far-reaching Wisdom help Thou Me
Fast in the Hand of Sorrow! Help Thou Me,
For I am very wretched!" Then THE SAGE—
Oh Thou that err'st not from the Road of Right,
If but SALÁMÁN have not broke my Bond,
Nor lies beyond the Noose of my Firmán,
He quickly shall unload his Heart to me,
And I will find a Remedy for all."

26

Then THE SAGE counsell'd, and SALÁMÁN heard,
And drew the Wisdom down into his Heart;
And, sitting in the Shadow of the Perfect,
His Soul found Quiet under; sweet it seem'd,
Sweeping the Chaff and Litter from his own,
To be the very Dust of Wisdom's Door,
Slave of the Firmán of the Lord of Life.
Then THE SAGE marvell'd at his Towardness,
And wrought in Miracle in his own behalf.
He pour'd the Wine of Wisdom in his Cup,
He laid the Dew of Peace upon his lips;
And when Old Love return'd to Memory,
And broke in Passion from his Lips, THE SAGE,
Under whose waxing WILL Existence rose
Responsive, and, relaxing, waned again,
Raising a Phantom Image of ABSÁL,
Set it awhile before SALÁMÁN's Eyes,
Till, having sow'd the Seed of Quiet there,
It went again down to Annihilation.
But ever, for the Sum of his discourse,
THE SAGE would tell of a Celestial Love;
"ZUHRAH,"³⁷ he said, "the Lustre of the Stars
'Fore whom the Beauty of the Brightest wanes;

---

³⁷ The Planetary and Celestial Venus.

Who were she to reveal her perfect Beauty,
The Sun and Moon would craze; ZUHRAH," he said,
"The Sweetness of the Banquet—none in Song
Like Her—her Harp filling the Ear of Heaven,
That Dervish-dances at her Harmony."

SALÁMÁN listen'd, and inclin'd—again
Repeated, Inclination ever grew;
Until THE SAGE beholding in his Soul
The SPIRIT [38] quicken, so effectually
With ZUHRAH wrought, that she reveal'd herself
In her pure Beauty to SALÁMÁN's Soul,
And washing ABSÁL's Image from his Breast,
There reign'd instead. Celestial Beauty seen,
He left the Earthly; and, once come to know
Eternal Love, he let the Mortal go.

---

[38] THE SPIRIT.—"MAANY." The Mystical password of the Súfís, to express the Transcendental New Birth of The Soul.

27

The Crown of Empire how supreme a Lot!
The Throne of the Sultan how high!—But not
For All—None but the Heaven-ward Foot may
dare
To mount—The Head that touches Heaven to
wear!—
When the Belov'd of Royal Augury
Was rescued from the Bondage of ABSÁL,
Then he arose, and shaking off the Dust
Of that lost Travel, girded up his Heart,
And look'd with undefiled Robe to Heaven.
Then was His Head worthy to wear the Crown,
His Foot to mount the Throne. And then THE
SHAH
Summon'd the Chiefs of Cities and of States,
Summon'd the Absolute Ones who wore the
Ring,
And such a Banquet order'd as is not
For Sovereign Assemblement the like
In the Folding of the Records of the World.
No armed Host, nor Captain of a Host,
From all the Quarters of the World, but there;
Of whom not one but to SALÁMÁN did
Obeisance, and lifted up his Neck
To yoke it under his Supremacy.

Then THE SHAH crown'd him with the Golden
Crown,
And set the Golden Throne beneath his Feet,
And over all the Heads of the Assembly,
And in the Ears of all of them, his Jewels
With the Diamond of Wisdom cut and said:—

28

"My Son,[39] the Kingdom of The World is not
Eternal, nor the Sum of right Desire;
Make thou the Faith-preserving Intellect
Thy Counsellor; and considering TO-DAY
TO-MORROW'S Seed-field, ere That come to bear,
Sow with the Harvest of Eternity.
All Work with Wisdom hath to do—by that
Stampt current only; what Thyself to do
Art wise, that DO; what not, consult the Wise.
Turn not thy Face away from the old Ways,
That were the Canon of the Kings of Old;
Nor cloud with Tyranny the Glass of Justice;
But rather strive that all Confusion
Change by thy Justice to its opposite.
In whatsoever Thou shalt Take or Give
Look to the HOW; Giving and Taking still,
Not by the backward Counsel of the Godless,
But by the Law of FAITH increase and Give.
Drain not thy People's purse—the Tyranny
Which Thee enriches at thy Subjects' cost,
Awhile shall make Thee strong; but in the End

---

[39] MY SON.—one sees Jámí taking Advantage of his Allegorical Shah
to read a Lesson to the Real—whose Ears Advice, unlike Praise, scarce
ever reached unless obliquely. The Warning (and doubtless with good
Reason) is principally aimed at the Minister.

Shall bow thy Neck beneath a Double Burden.
The Tyrant goes to Hell—follow not Him—
Become not Thou the Fuel of its Fires.
Thou art a Shepherd, and thy Flock the People,
To save and not destroy; nor at their Loss
To lift Thyself above the Shepherd's calling.
For which is for the other, Flock or Shepherd?
And join with Thee true Men to keep the Flock.
Dogs, if you will—but Trusty—head in leash,
Whose Teeth are for the Wolf, not for the Lamb,
And least of all the Wolf's Accomplices,
Their Jaws blood-dripping from the Tyrant's
Shambles.
For Shahs must have Vizírs—but be they Wise
And Trusty—knowing well the Realm's Estate-
(For who eats Profit of a Fool? and least
A wise King girdled by a Foolish Council—)
Knowing how far to Shah and Subject bound
On either Hand—not by Extortion,
Nor Usury wrung from the People's purse,
Their Master's and their own Estates (to whom
Enough is apt enough to make them Rebel)
Feeding to such a Surplus as feeds Hell.
Proper in Soul and Body be They—pitiful
To Poverty—hospitable to the Saint—
Their sweet Access a Salve to wounded Hearts,

Their Vengeance terrible to the Evil Doer,
Thy Heralds through the Country bringing
Thee
Report of Good or Ill—which to confirm
By thy peculiar Eye—and least of all
Suffering Accuser also to be Judge—
By surest Steps builds up Prosperity."

29

EPILOGUE.

Under the Outward Form of any Story
An Inner Meaning lies—This Story now
Completed, do Thou of its Mystery
(Whereto the Wise hath found himself a way)
Have thy Desire—No Tale of I and THOU,
Though I and THOU be its Interpreters.[40]
What signifies THE SHAH? and what THE SAGE?
And what SALÁMÁN not of Woman born?
And what ABSÁL who drew him to Desire?
And what the KINGDOM that awaited him
When he had drawn his garment from her
Hand?
What means that FIERY PILE? and what THE
SEA?
And what that Heavenly ZUHRAH who at last
Clear'd ABSÁL from the Mirror of his Soul?
Learn part by part the Mystery from me;
All Ear from Head to Foot and Understanding
be.

---

[40] The Story is of 'Generals,' though enacted by 'Particulars.'

30

The Incomparable Creator, when this World
He did create, created First of All
The FIRST INTELLIGENCE[41]—First of a Chain
Of Ten Intelligences, of which the Last
Sole Agent is in this our Universe,
ACTIVE INTELLIGENCE so call'd; The One
Distributor of Evil and of Good,
Of Joy and Sorrow, Himself apart from MATTER,
In Essence and in Energy—his Treasure
Subject to no such Talisman—He yet
Hath fashion'd all that is—Material Form,
And Spiritual, sprung from HIM—by HIM
Directed all, and in his Bounty drown'd.

---

[41] These Intelligences are only another Form of the Neo-Platonic
Dæmones. The Neo-Platonists held that Matter and Spirit could have
no Intercourse—they were, as it were, 'incommensurate.' How then,
granting this premise, was Creation possible? Their answer was a kind
of gradual Elimination. God, the "Actus Purus," created an Œon; this
Œon created a Second; and so on, until the Tenth Œon was sufficiently
Material (as the Ten were in a continually descending Series), to affect
Matter, and so cause the Creation by giving to Matter the Spiritual
'Form.' Similarly, we have in Sufiism these Ten Intelligences in a
corresponding Series, and for the same End. There are Ten
Intelligences, and Nine Heavenly Spheres, of which the Ninth is the
Uppermost Heaven, appropriated to the First Intelligence; the Eighth,
that of the Zodiac, to the Second; the Seventh, Saturn, to the Third; the
Sixth, Jupiter, to the Fourth; the Fifth, Mars, to the Fifth; the Fourth,
The Sun, to the Sixth; the Third, Venus, to the Seventh; the Second,
Mercury, to the Eighth; the First, The Moon, to the Ninth; and THE
EARTH is the peculiar Sphere of the TENTH, or lowest Intelligence,
celled THE ACTIVE.

Therefore is He that Firmán-issuing SHAH
To whom the World was subject. But because
What He distributes to the Universe
Himself from still a Higher Power receives,
The Wise, and all who comprehend aright,
Will recognise that Higher in THE SAGE.

His the PRIME SPIRIT that, spontaneously
Projected by the TENTH INTELLIGENCE,
Was from no Womb of MATTER reproduced
A Special Essence called THE SOUL—a CHILD
Fresh sprung from Heaven in Raiment
undefiled
Of Sensual Taint, and therefore call'd SALÁMÁN.
And who ABSÁL?—The Lust-adoring Body,
Slave to the Blood and Sense—through whom
THE SOUL,
Although the Body's very Life it be,
Does yet imbibe the Knowledge and Desire
Of Things of SENSE; and these united thus
By such a Tie GOD only can unloose,
BODY and SOUL are Lovers Each of other.
What is THE SEA on which He sail'd?—The Sea
Of Animal Desire—the Sensual Abyss,
Under whose Water lie a World of Being
Swept far from God in that Submersion.

جلال‌الدین محمد رومی

And wherefore was it ABSÁL in that Isle
Deceived in her Delight, and that SALÁMÁN
Fell short of his Desire?—That was to show
How PASSION tires, and how with Time begins
The Folding of the Carpet of Desire

And what the turning of SALÁMÁN's Heart
Back to THE SHAH, and looking to the Throne
Of Pomp and Glory? What but the Return
Of the Lost SOUL to its true Parentage,
And back from Carnal Error looking up
Repentant to its Intellectual Throne.

What is THE FIRE?—Ascetic Discipline,
That burns away the Animal Alloy,
Till all the Dross of MATTER be consumed,
And the Essential Soul, its raiment clean
Of Mortal Taint, be left. But forasmuch
As any Life-long Habit so consumed,
May well recur a Pang for what is lost,
Therefore THE SAGE set in SALÁMÁN's Eyes
A Soothing Phantom of the Past, but still
Told of a Better Venus, till his Soul
She fill'd, and blotted out his Mortal Love.

For what is ZUHRAH?—That Divine Perfector,
Wherewith the Soul inspired and all arrayed

In Intellectual Light is Royal blest,
And mounts The Throne, and wears
The Crown, and Reigns
Lord of the Empire of Humanity.

This is the Meaning of This Mystery
Which to know wholly ponder in thy Heart,
Till all its ancient Secret be enlarged.
Enough—The written Summary I close,
And set my Seal:

THE TRUTH GOD ONLY KNOWS.

LIFE OF JÁMÍ
By
Edward FitzGerald

[I hope the following disproportionate Notice of Jámí's Life will be amusing enough to excuse its length. I found most of it . . . in Rosenzweig's "Biographische Notizen" of Jámí, from whose own, and Commentator's, Works it purports to be gathered. E.F.]

NÚRUDDÍN ABDURRAHMAN, Son of Maulána Nizamuddin Ahmed, and descended on the Mother's side from One of the Four great "FATHERS" of Islamism, was born A.H. 817, A.D. 1414, in Jám, a little Town of Khorásan, whither (according to the Heft Aklím—"Seven Climates") his Grandfather had migrated from Desht of Ispahán, and from which the Poet ultimately took his Takhalus, or Poetic name, JÁMÍ. This word also signifies "A Cup;" wherefore, he says, "Born in Jám, and dipt in the "Jam" of Holy Lore, for a double reason I must be called JÁMÍ in the Book of Song." He was celebrated afterwards in other Oriental Titles—"Lord of Poets"—"Elephant of

Wisdom," &c., but often liked to call himself "The Ancient of Herát," where he mainly resided.

When Five Years old he received the name of Núruddín—the "Light of Faith," and even so early began to show the Metal, and take the Stamp that distinguished him through Life. In 1419, a famous Sheikh, Khwájah Mehmed Parsa, then in the last year of his Life, was being carried through Jám. "I was not then Five Years old," says Jámí, "and my Father, who with his Friends went forth to salute him, had me carried on the Shoulders of one of the Family and set down before the Litter of the Sheikh, who gave a Nosegay into my hand. Sixty years have passed, and methinks I now see before me the bright Image of the Holy Man, and feel the Blessing of his Aspect, from which I date my after Devotion to that Brotherhood in which I hope to be enrolled."

So again, when Mauláná Fakhruddín Loristani had alighted at his Mother's house— "I was then so little that he set me upon his Knee, and with his Fingers drawing the Letters of 'Alí' and 'Omar' in the Air, laughed delightedly to hear me spell them. He also by his Goodness sowed in my Heart the Seed of his Devotion, which has grown to Increase within me—in which I hope to live, and in which to die. Oh God! Dervish let me live, and Dervish die; and in the Company of the Dervish do Thou quicken me to Life again!"

Jámí first went to a School at Herát; and afterward to one founded by the Great Timúr at Samarcand. There he not only outstript his Fellows in the very Encyclopaedic Studies of Persian Education, but even puzzled the Doctors in Logic, Astronomy, and Theology; who, however, with unresenting Gravity welcomed him—"Lo! a new Light added to our Galaxy!"—In the wider Field of Samarcand he might have liked to remain; but Destiny liked otherwise, and a Dream recalled him to Herát. A Vision of the Great Súfi Master there, Mehmed Saaduddín Kaschgari, of the Nakhsbend Order of Dervishes, appeared to him in his Sleep, and bade him return to One who would satisfy all Desire. Jámí went back to Herát; he saw the Sheikh discoursing with his Disciples by the Door of the Great Mosque; day after day passed by without daring to present himself; but the Master's Eye was upon him; day by day draws him nearer and nearer—till at last the Sheikh announces to those about him—"Lo! this Day have I taken a Falcon in my Snare!"

Under him Jámí began his Súfi Noviciate, with such Devotion, and under such Fascination from the Master, that going, he tells us, but for one Summer Day's Holiday into the Country, one single Line was enough to "lure the Tassel-gentle back again;"

"Lo! here am I, and Thou look'st on the Rose!"

By and bye he withdraws, by course of Súfi Instruction, into Solitude so long and profound, that on his Return to Men he has almost lost the Power of Converse with them. At last, when duly taught, and duly authorized to teach as Súfi Doctor, he yet will not, though solicited by those who had seen such a Vision of Him as had drawn Himself to Herát; and not till the Evening of his Life is he to be seen with White hairs taking that place by the Mosque which his departed Master had been used to occupy before.

Meanwhile he had become Poet, which no doubt winged his Reputation and Doctrine far and wide through Nations to whom Poetry is a vital Element of the Air they breathe.

"A Thousand times," he says, "I have repented of such Employment; but I could no more shirk it than one can shirk what the Pen of Fate has written on his Forehead—As Poet I have resounded through the World; Heaven filled itself with my Song, and the Bride of Time adorned her Ears and Neck with the Pearls of my Verse, whose coming Caravan the Persian Hafíz and Saadi came forth gladly to salute, and the Indian Khosrú and Hasan hailed as a Wonder of the World. The Kings of India and Rúm greet me by Letter: the Lords of Irák and Tabríz load me with Gifts; and what shall I say of those of Khorasán, who drown me in an Ocean of Munificence?"

This, though Oriental, is scarcely Bombast. Jámí was honoured by Princes at home and abroad, and at the very time they were cutting one another's Throats; by his own

Sultan Abou Saïd; by Hasan Beg of Mesopotamia—"Lord of Tabríz"—by whom Abou Saïd was defeated, dethroned, and slain; by Mahomet II. of Turkey—"King of Rúm"—who in his turn defeated Hasan; and lastly by Husein Mirza Baikara, who extinguished the Prince whom Hasan had set up in Abou's Place at Herát. Such is the House that Jack builds in Persia.

As Hasan Beg, however—the USUNCASSAN of old European Annals—is singularly connected with the present Poem, and with probably the most important event in Jámí's Life, I will briefly follow the Steps that led to that as well as other Princely Intercourse.

In A.H. 877, A.D. 1472, Jámí set off on his Pilgrimage to Mecca. He, and, on his Account, the Caravan he went with, were honourably and safely escorted through the intervening Countries by order of their several Potentates as far as Bagdad. There Jámí fell into trouble by the Treachery of a Follower he had reproved, and who (born 400 Years too soon) misquoted Jámí's Verse into disparagement of Ali, the Darling Imám of Persia. This getting wind at Bagdad, the thing was brought to solemn Tribunal, at which Hasan Beg's two Sons assisted. Jámí came victoriously off; his Accuser pilloried with a dockt Beard in Bagdad Marketplace: but the Poet was so ill pleased with the stupidity of those who believed the Report, that, standing in Verse upon the Tigris' side, he calls for a Cup of Wine to seal up Lips of whose Utterance the Men of Bagdad were unworthy.

After four months' stay there, during which he visits at Helleh the Tomb of Ali's Son, Husein, who had fallen at Kerbela, he sets forth again—to Najaf, where he says his Camel sprang forward at sight of Ali's own Tomb—crosses the Desert in 22 days, meditating on the Prophet's Glory, to Medina; and so at last to Mecca, where, as he sang in a Ghazal, he went through all Mahommedan Ceremony with a Mystical Understanding of his Own.

He then turns Homeward: is entertained for 45 days at Damascus, which he leaves the very Day before the Turkish Mahomet's Envoys come with 5000 Ducats to carry him to Constantinople. Arriving at Amida, the Capital of Mesopotamia (Diyak bakar), he finds War broken out in full Flame between that Mahomet and Hasan Beg, King of the Country, who has Jámí honourably escorted through the dangerous Roads to Tabríz; there receives him in Diván, "frequent and full" of Sage and Noble (Hasan being a great Admirer of Learning), and would fain have him abide at Court awhile. Jámí, however, is intent on Home, and once more seeing his aged Mother—for *he* is turned of Sixty!—and at last touches Herát in the Month of Schaaban, 1473, after the Average Year's absence.

This is the HASAN, "in Name and Nature *Handsome*" (and so described by some Venetian Ambassadors of the Time), of whose protection Jámí speaks in the Preliminary Vision of this Poem, which he dedicates to Hasan's Son, Yacúb Beg: who, after the due murder of an Elder Brother, succeeded to the Throne; till all the Dynasties of "Black and White Sheep" together were swept away a few years after by Ismael, Founder of the Sofí Dynasty in Persia.

Arrived at home, Jámí finds Husein Mirza

Baikara, last of the Timúridae, fast seated there; having probably slain ere Jámí went the Prince whom Hasan had set up; but the date of a Year or Two may well wander in the Bloody Jungle of Persian History. Husein, however, receives Jámí with open Arms; Nisamuddín Ali Schír, his Vizir, a Poet too, had hailed in Verse the Poet's Advent from Damascus as "The Moon rising in the West;" and they both continued affectionately to honour him as long as he lived.

Jámí sickened of his mortal Illness on the 13th of Moharrem, 1492—a Sunday. His Pulse began to fail on the following Friday, about the Hour of Morning Prayer, and stopped at the very moment when the Muezzin began to call to Evening. He had lived Eighty-one years.

Sultan Husein undertook the Burial of one whose Glory it was to have lived and died in Dervish Poverty; the Dignities of the Kingdom followed him to the Grave; where twenty days afterward was recited in presence of the Sultan and his Court an Eulogy composed by the Vizir, who also laid the first Stone of a Monument to his Friend's Memory—

the first Stone of "Tarbet'i Jámi," in the Street of
Mesched, a principal Thoro'fare of the City of
Herát. For, says Rosenzweig, it must be kept in
mind that Jámi was reverenced not only as a
Poet and Philosopher, but as a Saint also; who
not only might work a Miracle himself, but
leave the Power lingering about his Tomb. It
was known that once in his Life, an Arab, who
had falsely accused him of selling a Camel he
knew to be mortally unsound, had very shortly
after died, as Jámi had predicted, and on the
very selfsame spot where the Camel fell. And
that Libellous Rogue at Bagdad—he, putting
his hand into his Horse's Nose-bag to see if
"das Thier" has finisht his Corn, had his Fore-
finger bitten off by the same—"von demselben
der Zeigefinger abgebissen"—of which
"Verstümmlung" he soon died—I suppose, as
he ought, of Lock jaw.

The Persians, who are adepts at much
elegant Ingenuity, are fond of commemorating
Events by some analogous Word or Sentence
whose Letters, cabalistically corresponding to
certain Numbers, compose the Date required.
In Jámí's case they have hit upon the word
"Kas," A Cup, whose signification brings his

own name to Memory, and whose relative Letters make up his 81 years. They have *Taríks* also for remembering the Year of his Death: Rosenzweig gives some; but Ouseley the prettiest, if it will hold:—

Dúd az Khorásán bar ámed—"The smoke" of Sighs "went up from Khorásán." No Biographer, says Rosenzweig cautiously, records of Jámí that he had more than one Wife (Grand-daughter of his Master Sheikh) and Four Sons; which, however, are Five too many for the Doctrine of this Poem. Of the Sons, Three died Infant; and the Fourth (born to him in very old Age), and for whom he wrote some Elementary Tracts, and the more famous "Beharistan" lived but a few years, and was remembered by his Father in the Preface to his Chiradnameh Iskander—a book of Morals, which perhaps had also been begun for the Boy's Instruction.

Of Jámí's wonderful Fruitfulness— "bewunderungswerther Fruchtbarkeit"—as Writer, Rosenzweig names Forty-four offsprings—the Letters of the word "Jám" completing by the aforesaid process that very

Number. But Shár Khán Lúdi in his "Memoirs of the Poets," says Ouseley, counts him Author of *Ninety-nine* Volumes of Grammar, Poetry, and Theology, which "continue to be universally admired in all parts of the Eastern World, Iran, Turin, and Hindustan"—copied some of them into precious Manuscript, illuminated with Gold and Painting, by the greatest Penmen and Artists of the Time; one such—the "Beharistan"—said to have cost Thousands of Pounds—autographed as one most precious treasure of their Libraries by two Sovereign Descendants of TIMÚR upon the Throne of Hindustan; and now reposited away from "the Drums and Tramplings" of Oriental Conquest in the tranquil Seclusion of an English Library.

Of these Ninety-nine, or Forty-four Volumes few are known, and none except the Present and one other Poem ever printed, in England, where the knowledge of Persian might have been politically useful. The Poet's name with us is almost solely associated with "YÚSUF AND ZULAIKHA," which, with the other two I have mentioned, count Three of the Brother Stars of that Constellation into which Jámí, or his Admirers, have clustered his Seven best

Mystical Poems under the name of "Heft Aurang"—those "Seven Thrones" to which we of the West and North give our characteristic Name of "Great Bear" and "Charles's Wain."

He must have enjoyed great Favour and Protection from his Princes at home, or he would hardly have ventured to write so freely as in this Poem he does of Doctrine which exposed the Súfí to vulgar abhorrence and Danger. Hafíz and others are apologized for as having been obliged to veil a Divinity beyond what "The Prophet" dreamt of under the Figure of Mortal Cup and Cup-bearer. Jámí speaks in Allegory too, by way of making a palpable grasp at the Skirt of the Ineffable; but he also dares, in the very thick of Mahommedanism, to talk of Reason as sole Fountain of Prophecy; and to pant for what would seem so Pantheistic an Identification with the Deity as shall blind him to any distinction between Good and Evil. 1

I must not forget one pretty passage of Jámí's Life. He had a nephew, one Maulána Abdullah, who was ambitious of following his Uncle's Footsteps in Poetry. Jámí first dissuaded him; then, by way of trial whether he had a Talent as well as a Taste, bid him imitate Firdusi's Satire on Shah Mahmúd. The Nephew did so well, that Jámí then encouraged him to proceed; himself wrote the first Couplet of his First (and most noted) Poem—Laila & Majnun.

This Book of which the Pen has now laid the Foundation,
May the diploma of Acceptance one day befall it,—

and Abdallah went on to write that and four other Poems which Persia continues and multiplies in fine Manuscript and Illumination to the present day, remembering their Author under his Takhalus of HÁTIFI—"The Voice from Heaven" and Last of the so reputed Persian Poets.

EDWARD FITZGERALD

H.D. Greaves

Edward FitzGerald was born on March 31st, 1809, the seventh of eight children born to John Purcell and Mary Frances FitzGerald. John Purcell assumed the arms and name of FitzGerald upon the death of his father-in-law, which explains why Edward carries the name FitzGerald rather than Purcell. The FitzGeralds were one of the wealthiest families in England.

Edward entered Trinity College, Cambridge, in 1826, and obtained, with remarkable indolence, a degree in 1830, after which he travelled to France. Independently wealthy and lacking ambition, though by no means a spendthrift, he spent his time reading, writing, travelling, and visiting friends, many of whom were prominent philosophers and writers, most notably Alfred Lord Tennyson.

In 1856, when nearly fifty, he married a spinster of forty-eight. From the beginning, the marriage was a disaster. Much has been made of this, but ultimately what we have here are two middle-aged people of entirely different temperament and habits, each set in their ways, and utterly refusing to change. After six months of misery, they separated permanently.

FitzGerald loved the sea and purchased a small yacht, which he christened *Scandal.* Late in his life, he entered into a fishing partnership with a good friend who was a fisherman. Unfortunately, this venture was plagued with difficulties and eventually abandoned.

Disillusioned with Christianity, FitzGerald stopped attending church, which caused the pastor of the local parish to call, with the intent of censuring him. Instead, FitzGerald severely admonished the pastor, quickly showed him the door, and told him not to return.

Edward FitzGerald died peacefully in his sleep on June 14th, 1883. On his grave, which is located in the churchyard of St Michael & All Angels, Boulge, Suffolk, England, there grows a rose tree, the hips for which came from the rose tree that grew on the grave of Omar Khayyám in Naishápúr, picked there in 1884 by William Simpson, and nurtured in Kew Gardens prior to planting on FitzGerald's grave in 1893. In 1972, six more rose trees were planted at his grave.

THE MAJOR WORKS
OF EDWARD FITZGERALD

1831   The Meadows of Spring

1849   Memoir of Bernhard Barton

1850   Salámán and Absál, an Allegory translated from the Persian of Jámi

1851   Euphranor, A Dialogue on Youth

1852   Polonius, A Collection of Wise Saws and Modern Instances

      Six Dramas of Calderon, freely translated

1859   Rubáiyát Of Omar Khayyám (First Edition)

1865   The Mighty Magician, Such Stuff as Dreams are made of

1868   Rubáiyát Of Omar Khayyám (Second Edition)

      The Two Generals

1872 Rubáiyát Of Omar Khayyám (Third
Edition)

1876 Agamemnon

1879 Rubáiyát Of Omar Khayyám (Fourth
Edition), together with Salámán and
Absál)

1879 Readings in Crabbe, Tales of the Hall

1880 The Downfall and Death of King
Oedipus

1889 Rubáiyát Of Omar Khayyám (Fifth
Edition)

1914 Dictionary of Madame de Sévigné

ABOUT H.D. GREAVES

Close friends compare H.D. Greaves to the Phoenix, the bird that always rises from its own ashes. A Trinidad author, now in his eighties, he continues to live and work in Port of Spain.

H.D.'s books are available on Amazon's Kindle, and on Amazon's KDP Print on Demand.

MANDRAGORA - *A Ribald and Irreverent Tale from the Italian Renaissance*

CLIZIA - *A Tale of Scandalous Surprises from the Italian Renaissance*

POONKY DOODLES - *A Novel of Growth and Survival*

OF BLISS AND GRANTED WISHES - *A True Story told as a Novel*

THE NARRATIVE VOICE - *Nine Intriguing Stories and a Novella*

SEVEN PLAYS - *An Anthology*

DRAMATIS PERSONAE - *Poems of Comedy and Tragedy*

MANDRAKE AMOROSO - *An Italian Renaissance Comedy Inspired by Niccolò Machiavelli's La Mandragola*

H.D. GREAVES LARGE PRINT BOOKS

Available in high quality Paperbacks

THE WITCH OF TABAQUITE - A NOVELLA

TURANDOT'S UKULELE

A SLIGHT CONTRETEMPS

GOING BAREFOOT INTO PARADISE

BARBARA NOM DE PLUME

CLEOPATRUS EXCAPTIVUS

THE TALE OF THE JAPANESE EMBASSY'S
MOST ESTEEMED CHEF

A CUCKOO'S LAMENT

THE KEEPER and GIFTS

PREFACED AND EDITED BY
H.D. GREAVES:

The Rubáiyát of Omar Khayyám
Translated into English Verse
By
Edward FitzGerald

Salámán and Absál
An Allegory by Jami
Translated from the Persian
By
Edward FitzGerald

Euphranor
A Dialogue on Youth
By
Edward FitzGerald

A Christmas Carol
Personally Abridged for Performance
By
Charles Dickens

WEBSITE

hdgreavesauthor.wix.com/caribbeanwriter